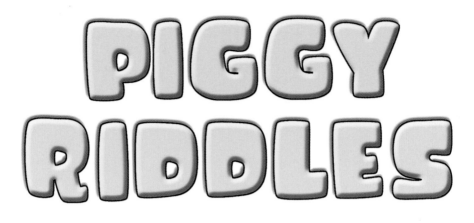

PIGGY RIDDLES

by Katy Hall and Lisa Eisenberg

pictures by Renée Andriani

Dial Books for Young Readers • New York

Published by Dial Books for Young Readers
A division of Penguin Young Readers Group
345 Hudson Street
New York, New York 10014
Text copyright © 2004 by Kate McMullan and Lisa Eisenberg
Pictures copyright © 2004 by Renée Andriani
Manufactured in China on acid-free paper
The Dial Easy-to-Read logo is a registered trademark of
Dial Books for Young Readers, a division of Penguin Young Readers Group
® TM 1,162,718.

10 9 8 7 6 5 4 3 2 1

Library of Congress Cataloging-in-Publication Data
Hall, Katy.
Piggy riddles / by Katy Hall and Lisa Eisenberg;
pictures by Renée Andriani.
    p.   cm.
Summary: Thirty-four riddles about pigs, including
"What did the piggy's fairy godmother do?
She grunted him three wishes" and "How do sty-lish sows
wear their hair? In pig-tails."
ISBN 0-8037-2855-7
1. Riddles, Juvenile. 2. Swine—Juvenile humor.
[1. Pigs—Humor. 2. Riddles. 3. Jokes.]
I. Eisenberg, Lisa. II. Andriani, Renée, ill. III.Title.
PN6371.5 .H34863 2004
818'.5402—dc21   2002014626

The art was drawn with pen and ink,
then scanned and colored in Photoshop.

In memory of the pig
—L.E.

For Charlotte Steiner, who tells a great riddle
—K.H.

For Steven J. DaSilva
—R.A.

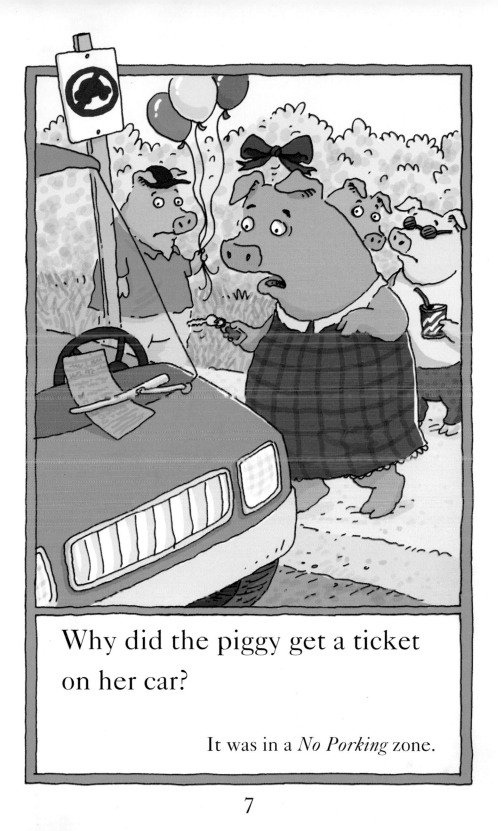

Why did the piggy get a ticket on her car?

It was in a *No Porking* zone.

What's large, pink, and hairy,
and stomps around the swamp?

Pig Foot.

What do you call it when a piggy takes a bath?

Hogwash!

Why did the piggy help the sow across the street?

He was a member of the Boy Snouts of Hamerica.

How did the piglet get his
sister in trouble?

He squealed on her.

How do pigs sing the scales?

Do, re, mi, fa, *sow*, la, ti, do.

What position did the piggy
play on the baseball team?

Snort stop.

Why did the pig get kicked out of his apartment?

He forgot to pay the runt!

What did Professor Hogg see
when she looked through her
telescope?

The Pig Dipper.

What was the hog doing in the kitchen?

He was bacon!

Where do piggies ride the
bumper cars?

At the amusement pork.

17

How do pigs get to the
hospital?

By *ham*-bulance.

What game do little piggies
love to play?

Wallow the leader!

Why did the piglet bring
flowers to the sow?

It was *Mud*-ders' Day.

Why did the piglet eat three
whole pizzas?

He was trying to make a hog of himself.

What do you call a piggy who steals things?

A *ham*burglar

What do you get when you
cross a pig and a canary?

A *ham*mingbird!

What does Lady Pigge carry
when she has the sniffles?

Her oink-erchief.

Where do rich piggies live?

On *Pork* Avenue.

What do you call pigs who write each other notes?

Pen pals.

Why were all the piglets
squealing in the carriage?

They were a *litter* bit squashed.

What is a piggy's favorite movie?

The Sow*nd of Music.*

Why was the boar always bragging?

He thought he was a pig shot.

What did the piggy's fairy
godmother do?

She grunted him three wishes.

What is a piggy's favorite rock and roll song?

"Twist and Snout."

How did the farmer find his missing pig?

He tractor down!

Where does a city pig live?

In a sty-scraper.

How do you know if a piggy
likes the roller coaster?

She gives it her *squeal* of approval!

What do piggies practice in karate class?

Pork chops.

How do sty-lish sows wear
their hair?

In pig-tails.

Why was the pig blocking traffic?

He was a road hog!

Why were the piggies yawning
in class?

Their teacher was a big boar!